For my lovely wife, Sharon

Henry Holt and Company, LLC
Publishers since 1866
175 Fifth Avenue
New York, New York 10010
www.HenryHoltKids.com

Henry Holt® is a registered trademark of Henry Holt and Company, LLC.

Distributed in Canada by H. B. Fenn and Company Ltd.

Library of Congress Cataloging-in-Publication Data
Andreasen, Dan. The treasure bath / Dan Andreasen. — 1st ed.
p. cm.
"Christy Ottaviano Books."
Summary: A wordless picture book in which a young boy
explores a creature-filled world beneath the bubbles in his bathtub.
ISBN-13: 978-0-8050-8686-7
ISBN-10: 0-8050-8686-2
[1. Baths—Fiction. 2. Imagination—Fiction. 3. Stories without words.] I. Title.
PZ7.A55915Tre 2009 [E]—dc22 2008038224

First Edition—2009
The artist used oil on bristol board to create the illustrations for this book.
Printed in China on acid-free paper. ∞

1 3 5 7 9 10 8 6 4 2

THE TREASURE BATH

DAN ANDREASEN

Christy Ottaviano Books
Henry Holt and Company
New York

Cake
Mix

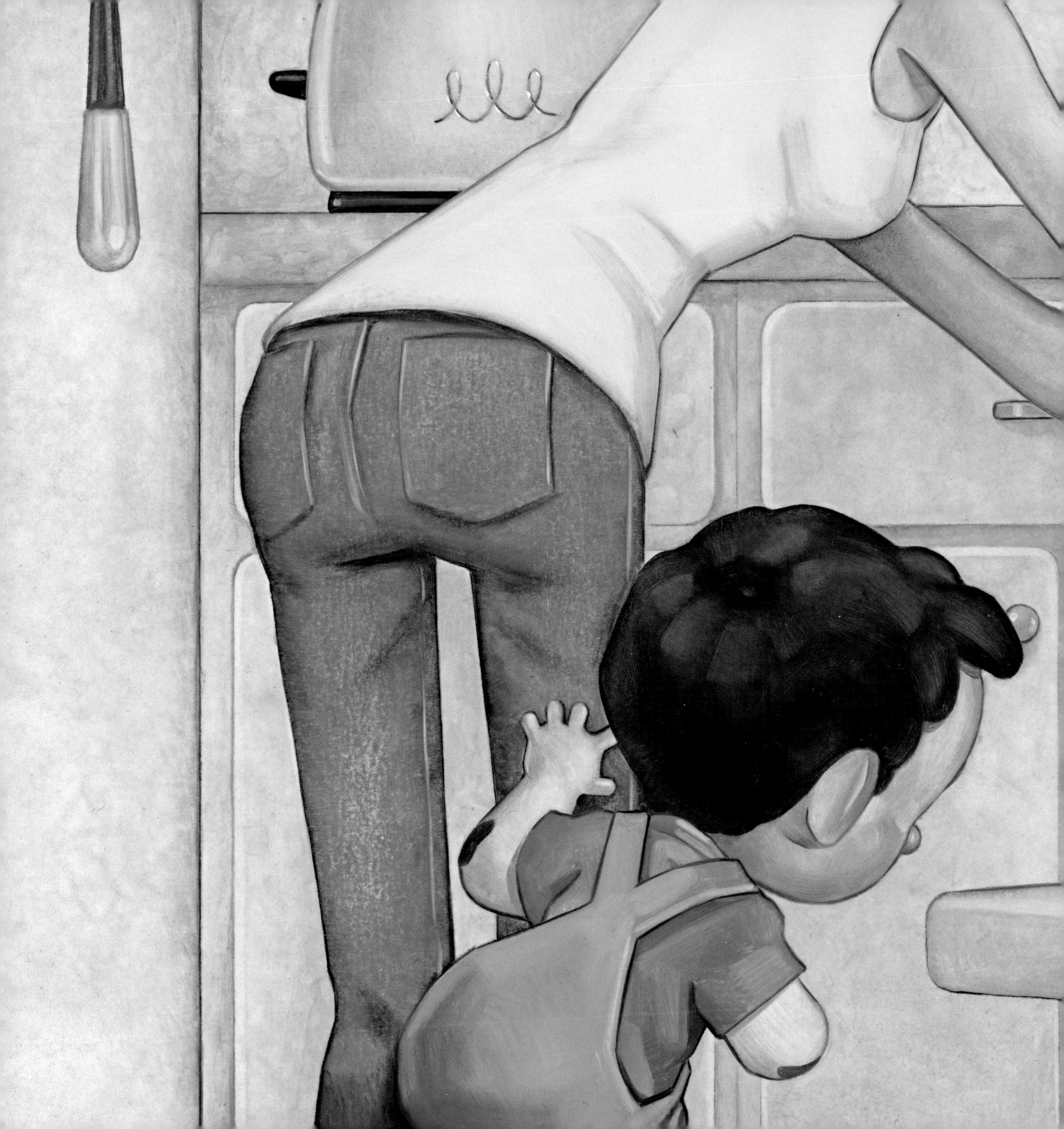

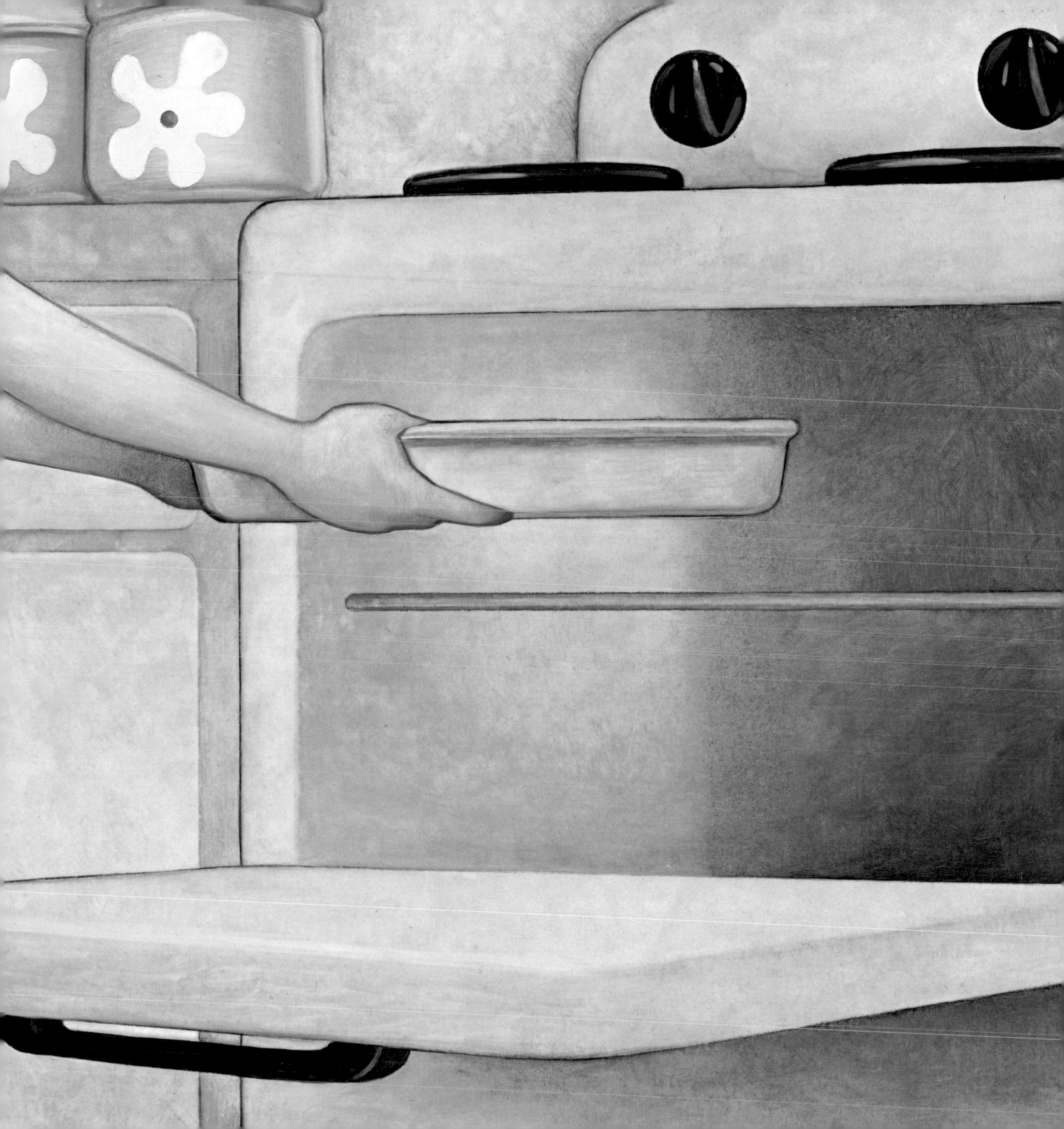

SOAP
SOAP
SOAP
SOAP
SHAMPOO
SOAP

SHAMP
SOAP

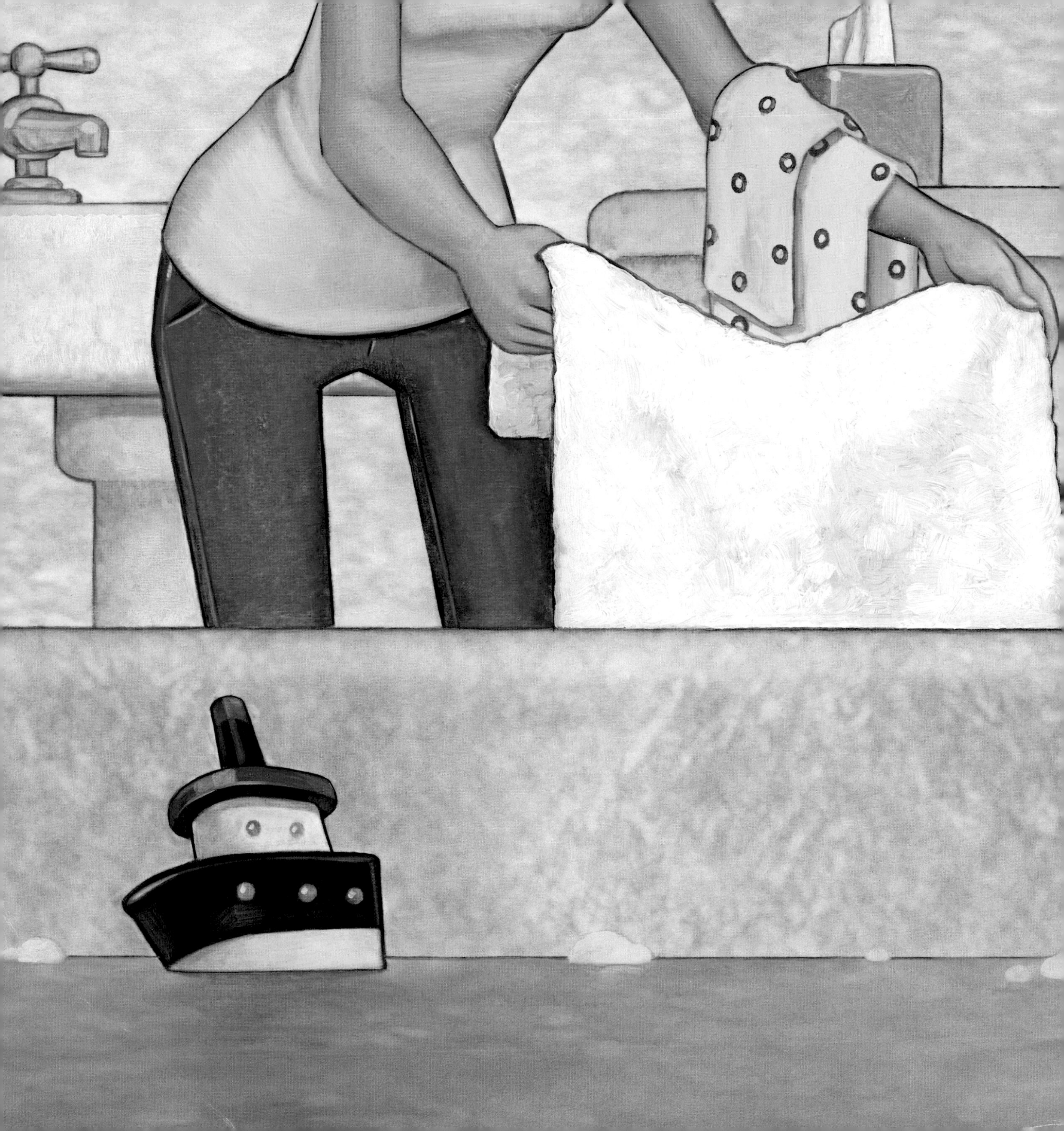